CU00860300

This book was sponsored by members of the QNI, Queens University, Northern Distributors, and other local businesses in Northern Ireland.

Written by Debbie Duncan and illustrated by Jennifer Davison

VICTOR
and the VIRUS

Sarah GRACE
PUBLISHING

First published 2021 by Sarah Grace Publishing
an imprint of Malcolm Down Publishing ltd.
www.sarahgracepublishing.co.uk

24 23 22 21   7 6 5 4 3 2 1

British Library Cataloguing in Publication Data
A catalogue record for this book is available
from the British Library.

ISBN 978-1-912863-93-8

Cover and Illustrations by Jennifer Davison
Art direction by Sarah Grace

Printed in the UK

Acknowledgements

This book is dedicated to my fabulous colleagues at Queens University.

Contents

Introduction   9

Chapter 1:   The accident   11

Chapter 2:   The hospital visit   19

Chapter 3:   What happened next   25

Chapter 4:   Peter and the pandemic   29

Chapter 5:   What You Can Do next   33

About the Series

The Story

Introduction

Many of us have an idea of what we want to do when we are older. Some people have no idea what they want to do. They may work it out as they grow up or meet people who do amazing jobs and they want to do them too.

This is the story of Victor who ended up in hospital with a broken arm, met some amazing people and decided that when he grew up he would become a nurse.

Chapter One

The accident

Victor was eight years old when he fell off his bike. It happened to him quite a lot but this time he ended up in hospital!

Victor was one of the tallest in his class. His friends called him Vic but he didn't like it as it reminded him of the name of the smelly stuff his mum would put under his nose when he had a cold. He had quite a few friends but he knew some of them were friendly because his uncle who played football for Linfield football club. They were currently the champions of the Northern Ireland Football League. In fact, his uncle had scored the winning goal of the last match of the season. Victor didn't mind being popular for that reason as it meant he could talk about football all day. At least his friends listened to him. When he chatted to his mum about football she nodded her head as if she was interested but he knew she wasn't. She took him to his football matches and sat on the side line but she didn't understand the rules, no matter how many times he had tried to explain them.

One day, Victor was racing his bike through the forest near his house with his best friend and team mate Sam.

They had set themselves a challenge to see who could race down the path the quickest. It had been a little tricky as it had been raining, as it usually did where he lived.

As Victor speeded up he cycled straight into a large tree root. His front tyre stopped, wedged in the ground but Victor didn't stop. The force of the accident sent him flying over his handlebars and he landed with his arms outstretched to protect himself as he fell. It seemed as if time stood still as his whole body went flying over his bike that had stuck in the tree. All Victor could think about was, "this is going to hurt". He could see the muddy area he was going to land in. Then for what seemed like a few minutes everything went quiet.

Suddenly Sam rushed over, shouting something to him. Victor was lying face down in the mud, his cycle helmet took the force of the fall. He felt cold and sweaty. Then as he expected his wrists started throbbing. He tried to get up but it was muddy and he couldn't use his hands to prop himself up. Sam was down on his hands and knees asking Victor if he was okay.

"Man that was crazy", he said. "Are you okay? No you don't look okay". They eventually got Victor sitting up, both covered in mud. "I am going to get your mum" Sam said. He took his jacket off and put it under Victor's arms. "I'll cycle to your house – it will be quicker and I'll be back".

Although he was cold and his arms both throbbed like mad, Victor was glad he had a few minutes alone. His helmet lay battered beside him. He saw his bike, the front tyre wedged into the tree root, he looked at his arms which he couldn't move and he began to cry.

Can you think of a time when you had an accident? What kind of help did you need? Victor was so fortunate that he was wearing his cycle helmet or he could have had a serious head injury.

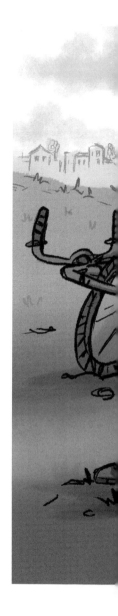

Chapter Two

The hospital visit

Sam was a good friend and he was soon back with help. Victor didn't remember a lot of what happened after that. He remembered being cold and very sore. In fact, he could not remember the last time he felt so much pain. It was more painful than Jack landing on him and squashing during his last football match! He remembered crying when his mum and dad arrived with Sam and that he was very embarrassed. He also remembered the loud siren of the ambulance stopping on the road near the track they were on. The paramedics put him in a chair and carried him up the track to the ambulance. His dad collected his bike and his mum went with him in the ambulance.

It was a bit scary at first as the ambulance was full of strange equipment. The ambulance crew were kind and told Victor what each piece of equipment was for. They took him to the hospital in the nearest town and on the way Victor fell asleep. He was still sore but had both arms in slings and that helped. Victor knew his mum was worried about him as she didn't say much and kept messing up his hair as she tried to clean the mud off his face.

It was Victor's first time in hospital and he was worried about what was going to happen. One of the team of nurses looking after him was a man called Mark. Mark, the nurse was so cool, he did funny magic tricks and told him silly jokes to stop Victor worrying while he waited for the doctor

Victor was taken to another room to have a photograph (x-ray) taken of his arms. After the photograph the doctor came into his room and told Victor and his mum that Victor had broken two bones in his arms. Mark, the nurse, explained that although Victor had broken two bones, they would probably heal quickly and he would get well soon. Nurse Mark told him Victor that he might even be well enough to make the last match of the season. Mark was kind and helped Victor understand what was happening and made him feel safe.

After his stay he could honestly say that there was nothing to be frightened about because he had Mark and other amazing nurses look after him.

Until Victor came to the hospital he had not known that men worked as nurses. When he got home later that night wearing his green and blue casts he told his dad about how Mark was so kind and caring. He shared some of Marks's silly jokes. Victor's Dad was also surprised that men worked as nurses.

There are many jobs that both men and women do. There are some jobs however that you find more men doing or more women doing. Chat about this with someone you trust. Why do you think that is the case?

Chapter Three

What happened next

It is amazing how often people ask you what you want to do when you grow up. Every time Victor saw his granny and grandad or his aunt and uncle they would all ask him what he wanted to be when he grew up. They didn't seem to want to know that he played football for his school, that he had good friends or what subjects he studied for his exams. Victor loved science, finding out how things work and he passed his exams with top marks.

Every day since he had met Mark, the kind nurse, Victor knew what he wanted to be when he grew up. He shared this with his friend Sam and the football team. They were surprised. When Victor came to choosing where he would study after his exams he knew his mum and dad wanted him to be a teacher. However, Victor knew what he wanted to study and he had to tell them.

One Sunday after his lunch, Victor told his mum and dad that he was going to university but not to study to be a teacher but to start studies to become a nurse. His dad was surprised and asked why? Victor explained that he had wanted to do nursing ever since he had met Mark, the nurse who looked after him and was kind to him when he was in hospital. He wanted to become a nurse to care for people who needed help, not just fix broken bones.

What do you think
is the difference
between a doctor
and a nurse?

Chapter Four

Victor and the pandemic

Victor was in the third year of his training when a virus – like flu began affecting people all around the world. They called it a pandemic. Victor still had several months to finish his studies before he could qualify as a nurse but his class were asked if they would volunteer to work on the wards caring for people that were sick with the virus.

Victor's arm was the first to go up when they asked for volunteers. He knew that he could make a difference to people's lives. He knew that he could help. Although his parents were worried about him, his mum and dad joined others on the street every Thursday night and clapped for those working with those who were sick with the virus. Victor knew that even his old football team were standing outside their doors on a Thursday night.

Victor's class were given extra lessons on how to protect themselves from the virus. They were taught how to wash their hands and put on their protective clothing. A few weeks later Victor found himself working in a ward that had people with the virus. There was an elderly man that he found himself chatting to when things were quiet on the ward.

Sometimes they would talk at night, and the man would talk about missing his family and friends. The patients were not allowed visitors Victor would always stop to tell the man a joke, to cheer him up but, the patient always knew the punch line. One-day Victor called into the mans' room to find him doing magic tricks. When Victor asked him where he had learnt the magic tricks. The elderly man laughed and said "From my son Mark, you know he is also a nurse". Victor remembered the kind nurse he had met so many years ago and now was his opportunity to return the kindness by looking after Mark's dad. As Victor walked home that night, he thought "What a small world, I am glad I am a nurse".

Chapter Five

What You Can Do next

If you would like to think about becoming a nurse, then there are a few things you can do.

- Talk to members of your family or family friends that are nurses.

- When you are older think about doing your work experience in health care.

- Look at the NHS website with an adult who can talk to you about it after.

Talk to your teachers at your school. They may even have some information about nursing that you can read. Once you are in secondary school there will be a careers advisor who should be able to help you.

For more information look at:
https://www.healthcareers.nhs.uk/we-are-the-nhs/nursing-careers